This Walt Disney Classic
Edition Belongs to:

_____

For information address:
Disney Editions
114 Fifth Avenue
New York, New York 10011-5690

Produced by:
Welcome Enterprises, Inc.
588 Broadway, Suite 303
New York, New York 10012

0-7868-5313-1

Library of Congress Cataloging-in-Publication
Data available upon request.

Printed in China

10 9 8 7 6 5 4 3 2 1

Walt Disney's
Santa's Toy Shop

Story adapted by Monique Peterson
Pictures by The Walt Disney Studios
Adapted by Al Dempster

A WELCOME BOOK

DISNEY
EDITIONS

New York

In a land way up north—at the tip of the North Pole—there's a magical place where winter stays the whole year long. Elves upon elves zigzag their skis through the snow on their way to a very special house—the Toy Shop of Mr. and Mrs. S. Claus.

The warm and cozy house is always filled with mouth-watering smells. In the kitchen, Mrs. Claus and the elves love to make cookies. First, they roll out the dough and cut out each shape. Then they put the cookies in the oven until they bake golden brown.

Santa loves to try the cookies. "Ho, ho, ho!" he chuckles. "I could eat these all night! But the elves are in the Toy Shop preparing for my flight!"

In Santa's Toy Shop, the elves are stitching and sprucing up the last of the dolls. . . .

They're laying out train tracks and painting
tunnels and cars. . . .

They're sawing wooden blocks, making toy parts,
and painting the squares on checkered game boards.

Then just when the elves finish making each ball,
block, truck, marble, and toy . . . they play with them all,
to make absolutely sure they're packed with good fun.

Not one detail is missed in Santa's Toy Shop. Santa himself personally makes sure to paint the very last smile on the very last doll.

Finally, the elves count up all the letters that have come to the North Pole. Then Santa checks his list of names—and checks it once again.

"Boys and girls have written me from all over the world!" Santa smiles and reads aloud.

"A doll for Janie . . . a fire truck for Saul . . . a race-car for Nenette . . . and for Jordan, a football! A bike for Nancy . . . new skates for Brett . . . And let's not forget Jerry's train set!"

When Santa is ready to gather all his goods, he opens his bag big and wide. The elves line up all the toys in the Toy Shop and send them down the long toy chute . . . one by one by one . . . until Santa's bag is filled to the top.

"Tonight is the big night," Santa says. "The biggest night of the year!"

"Christmas Eve!" chime the elves. "It's finally here!"

"At last, here I go!" Santa waves, with a twinkle in
his eye. "I must hurry and get the reindeer and pack
up my sleigh."

"The elves have done it for you," says Mrs. Claus,
waving Santa good night. "Have a great time as you
fly around the world tonight."

"Thank you, dear!" shouts Santa with joy. And sure enough, the elves have packed Santa's sleigh sky-high and hitched up all the reindeer, who are eager to fly.

So with a hearty "Ho, ho, ho!" Santa calls out the name of each reindeer. "And up, up, up we go!"

They fly across the sky and around the whole world,
stopping at the homes of everyone on his list.

Without making a noise (not even a peep!), Santa
lands on the rooftop. Then, with a wink of his eye
and a nod of his head, Santa slips down the chimney
as quick as a blink.

Santa loves finding notes . . . and treats of milk and cookies. As he reads each note, he smiles, knowing that he's making wishes come true.

At the very last house, Santa opens his big bag of toys. "At this house, we have a special request," Santa says to his elf. "The children who live here want us to add the Christmas magic that Santa knows best!"

Santa starts with the Christmas tree and adds candy canes, tinsel, ornaments, and lights. For a finish, he tops it with a shining star—big, blue, and bright.

He unpacks the electric train and sets up the station. With a nod of his head, he sends the train racing around the track.

Then, as quick as a flash, he sets up the blocks
and flies the toy plane . . . with that special magic
that only Santa has.

As Santa plays with each doll, he sings a final "Noel." And he says, "Now on Christmas morning the children will see there's Christmas magic in everything—from the tiniest toy to the tip of the tree."

Just before the break of dawn, Santa leaves the
very last town. He calls out to his reindeer, "Home
to Mrs. Claus by Christmas morn!"

While the children are still dreaming, Santa returns
to the North Pole—with his reindeer, elves, and
empty sleigh.

"How was your trip?" asks Mrs. Claus, greeting
Santa in the snow.

"Bundles of fun!" replies Santa, with a "Ho, ho, ho!"

Then Santa tells Mrs. Claus all about Christmas Eve—all the chimneys he dropped down, all the letters he read, and the special wish at the very last house.

"And right about now," Santa whispers in her ear, "all the boys and girls are waking up to find out that I've been there!"

When Christmas is over, Santa records all the children in his big book of names. Then he starts thinking about *next* Christmas, and everything he'll do . . . for each and every boy and girl . . . and especially for you!